THE
LITTLEST
ANGEL
EARNS HIS HALO

By
Ronald Kidd

Illustrated by
Rick Reinert

Dedicated To
Paul William Loscutoff

ideals®

Ideals Publishing Corporation
Milwaukee, Wisconsin

ISBN 0-8249-8078-6

Once upon a time, in the gleaming halls of heaven, there lived a small cherub known as the Littlest Angel. But he did more than just live there. He jumped there. He skipped there. He giggled and shouted and turned somersaults there.

The other angels, who
were most likely to ponder,
reflect, and muse, didn't know
what to make of him. So the
Littlest Angel spent most of his
time alone.

That didn't stop him from having fun, though. And fun was just what he was having one lovely spring day in the part of heaven known as the Elysian Fields. He was throwing his halo into the air, then watching it float back down, when all at once a breeze came up. Instead of floating down, his halo floated sideways and landed in the branch of a tree.

As he stood there wondering what to do, he saw a group of angels hurrying across the far side of the meadow. He called for help, but they were too busy to notice. Another group hurried by, and another, but no one saw him.

Just as the Littlest Angel was about to give up, he heard a new sound. It was a deep, rich voice humming a happy tune. The humming grew louder, and out of the nearby woods strode the Singer, also known as the Understanding Angel. He looked at the scene before him and immediately saw what was wrong.

Without missing a note, the Understanding Angel scooped up his young friend and held him high overhead. The Littlest Angel plucked his halo from the branch. When he looked at it, his eyes met with a sad sight. The halo was bent.

"I'm afraid you've got a problem there," said the Understanding Angel as he set his friend on the ground.

The Littlest Angel put the
halo back on his head. "I guess I
should get it fixed, huh?"
"I'd say so," replied the
Understanding Angel, "especially
since today is the big day."

"The big day?"

"Haven't you heard?" he asked. "The King is returning. That's why all the angels and archangels are so busy hurrying around. They want everything to be perfect for his arrival."

Eager to get ready, the Littlest Angel said a quick thank you and raced off. He went straight to the Halosmith, a strong, broad-shouldered angel who was hard at work in his shop just outside the Celestial City.

"Do you think you could find time to fix my halo?" the Littlest Angel asked him. "I want it to look just right when the King returns."

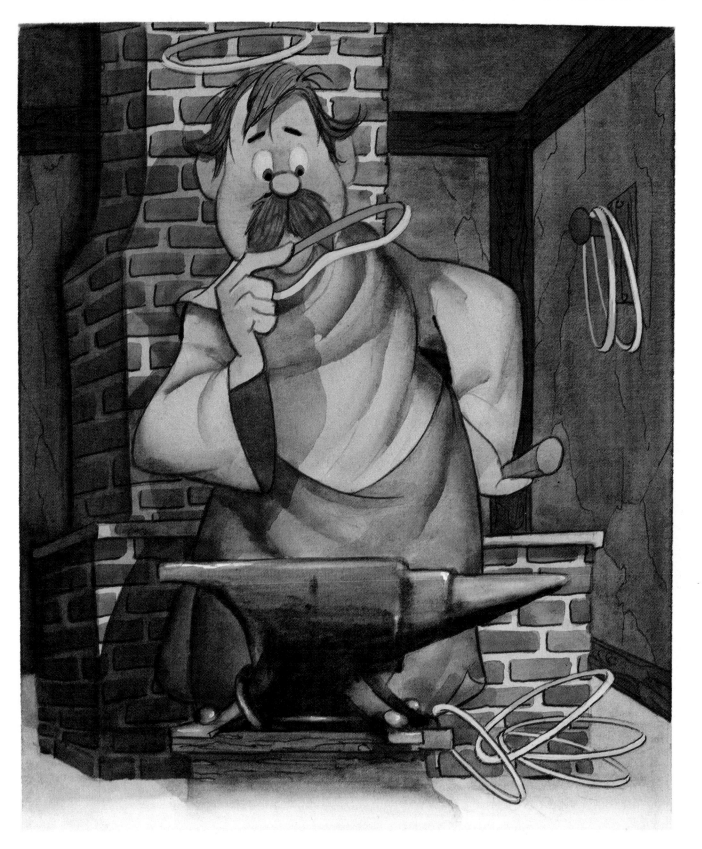

The Halosmith took one look at it and shook his head sadly. "I wish I could, but once a halo is bent, it can't be fixed."

"Then I'll just have to get a new one," declared the Littlest Angel.

"I'm afraid it's not that simple. You don't just get a new halo. You have to earn it. It's not easy, especially in one day."

"What can I do to earn it?" asked the Littlest Angel.

The Halosmith scratched his chin. "I suppose you could start by helping me. I'm polishing halos for the Patriarch Prophets, because they'll be the first to greet the King."

The Halosmith took his new helper over to a box of halos that were scuffed and scratched. He showed him how to polish the golden circles, then went to work, leaving the Littlest Angel by himself.

Whistling a heavenly tune, the Littlest Angel started polishing. But the work went slowly. At the rate he was going, he would never earn a new halo!

He looked around the shop, and there before his eyes was the answer to his problem: cans and cans of paint. Instead of polishing the halos, he would paint them. The job would go faster, and the Patriarch Prophets would get halos in every color of the rainbow!

A short time later, the Halosmith came back to check on his helper. The Littlest Angel proudly displayed his work. The Halosmith's eyes opened wide, and his face grew pale.

"Is anything wrong?" asked the Littlest Angel.

"You know," said the Halosmith in a funny, pinched voice, "I think maybe I should do this job by myself. Thanks anyway."

The Littlest Angel left the Halosmith's shop, wondering where to go next. As he walked along the path, he heard a flutter of wings overhead. He looked up just in time to see an angel hurtling straight toward him, out of control. He dived out of the way, and the angel hit the ground with a thud.

The angel, a plump woman with shaggy brown hair, shook her head and climbed unsteadily to her feet.

"Are you okay?" asked the Littlest Angel.

"Me?" she said. "Sure, I'm fine." She introduced herself as the Wingmaker and explained that to get ready for the King's return, the Heavenly Host had brought their wings to her for cleaning and a trim.

She flapped the wings on her back. "I was just taking this pair for a test flight. Guess they could use a few adjustments."

The Littlest Angel asked if she needed an assistant. In response, she led him back to her studio — on foot, just to be safe — and opened the door to reveal shelf after shelf of wings.

"If you really want to help," she said, "you could organize these wings by size. Start with the biggest, and work down to the smallest."

Happy at another chance to earn a new halo, the Littlest Angel got to work. He went from one side of the studio to the other, collecting the largest wings he could find. Since they were made of feathers, he was able to carry a big pile of them easily. Soon the pile reached over his head, almost to the ceiling.

He was crossing the room to get yet another pair of wings, when he tripped, and the pile began to sway. The next thing he knew, he was lying face-down under a mountain of feathers.

The Wingmaker pulled him out from under the pile and brushed him off. "Now that I think about it," she said as she showed him to the door, "maybe those wings don't need organizing after all."

Discouraged, the Littlest Angel wandered into the Celestial City. As he walked past the cathedral, he heard the sound of voices. He peeked through the window and saw the Heavenly Choir, hard at work practicing hymns for the King's return. Here was another chance to earn a new halo!

He slipped inside the cathedral and came up behind the choir. They were busy singing, and he joined right in. It was so much fun that he found himself singing louder and louder. Before he knew it, he had thrown back his head and was shouting at the top of his lungs. It was grand. It was glorious.

It was a solo.

Halfway through the second verse, he realized he was singing alone. The others had stopped and were staring at him.

"Sorry," he mumbled, "I was just trying to earn a new halo." They stared at him all the way out the door.

The Littlest Angel trudged down the Street of Guardian Angels. On each side of him, cherubs swept the pavement and washed down the sidewalks. In the distance he saw the Gate of Heaven, where the King would make his grand entrance in just a few short hours.

As he gazed at the big pearl-covered door, his heart leaped. At last he knew how to earn a new halo. It would be better than helping the Heavenly Choir or the Wingmaker or the Halosmith. He would help his friend the Gate Keeper prepare the gate!

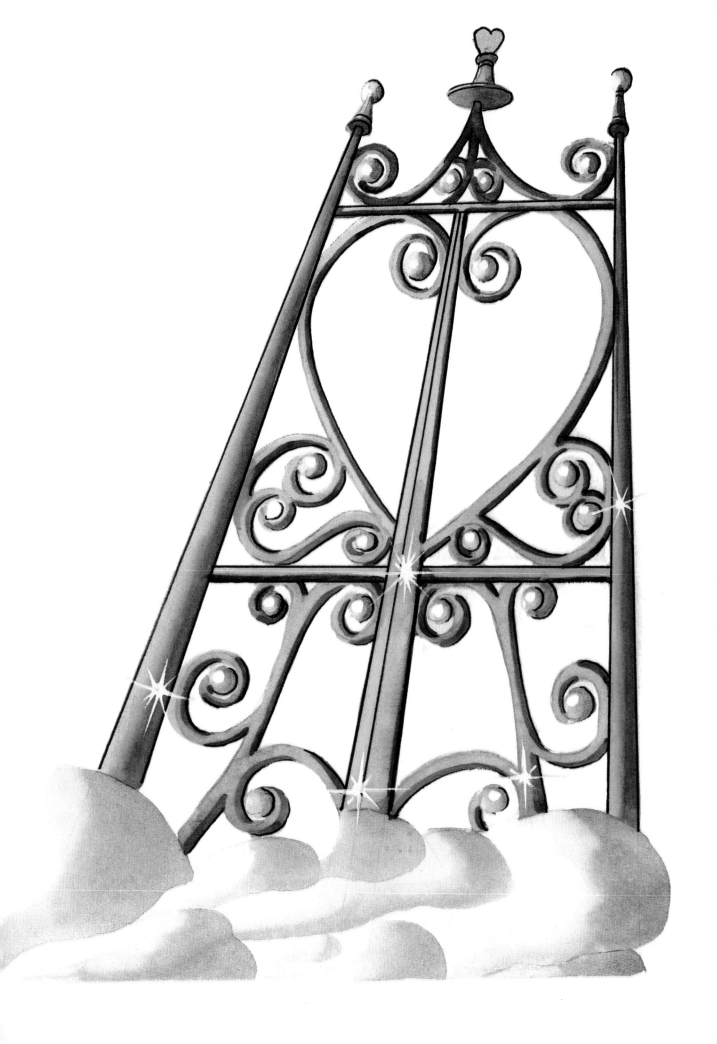

There was no sign of his friend, so the Littlest Angel decided to get started by himself. He opened the gate first one way, then another. He pushed. He pulled. He jumped on it and swung. He climbed over every inch of the gate, making sure it was ready for the King.

When the Gate Keeper returned, he found the Littlest Angel perched on top of the gate. "It looks like you've been busy," said the Gate Keeper.

"That's right," replied the Littlest Angel. "I've been helping you get ready for the King."

"Before you came," said the Gate Keeper, "I was busy, too."

"Doing what?" asked the Littlest Angel.

Eyeing the fingerprints and smudges that covered the pearly surface, he smiled sadly and said, "Cleaning the gate."

The Littlest Angel got up and crossed the field. Drawing near, he saw that the stranger's feet were bare, and he wore a simple robe. "Is anything wrong?" asked the cherub.

The stranger turned slowly around. He had a beard and deep brown eyes. "Oh, it's nothing," he said. "I've just arrived here, and I miss my friends."

"When I first came," said the Littlest Angel, "I felt the same way. But now I like it. It's my home, and these fields are my favorite place." He bent down, picked a bright yellow daisy, and handed it to the stranger.

The man smiled. He took the flower and fastened it to his robe. The two of them walked together through a meadow, watching the birds and butterflies and creatures of the field.

After a time, the stranger said, "I feel better now."

That was when the Littlest Angel remembered. "Oh, no," he blurted, "we've probably missed the King!"

He hurried to the Celestial City, with the stranger trailing behind. As the two of them approached, they could hear the crowd buzzing.

"Quick," said the Littlest Angel, "let's sneak through the gate." He went in first and motioned for the stranger to follow.

Inside there was lots of activity but no sign of the King. They had made it in time!

Then someone shouted, "He's here!" The angels grew quiet, and row by row they knelt along the Street of Guardian Angels. The Littlest Angel looked left and right but couldn't see the King. Then he glanced back toward the gate. Standing just inside was his companion.

One of the Patriarch Prophets walked up to the stranger.

"Welcome back, Lord," said the Prophet. He placed a crown on the stranger's head, then knelt in front of him.

The Littlest Angel backed away, sure that he had made his biggest mistake yet. His only thought was to disappear into the crowd and never come out again.

Then the stranger smiled. "Don't go," he said. "You're my friend." He stepped forward and took the Littlest Angel's hand. The young cherub stared up at him in wonder.

The stranger lifted the bent halo from the Littlest Angel's head. He took the bright yellow daisy from his own robe and placed it in the cherub's hair. As the crowd watched, the flower began to spin and glow until it had changed into a golden circle of light.

The Littlest Angel had earned a new halo.

Then the Heavenly Choir began to sing, and the crowd cheered. And the smallest cherub of all walked proudly into the city with his new friend, the man who was no longer a stranger, Jesus the King.